Exploring Shapes™

Polygons

Bonnie Coulter Leech

The Rosen Publishing Group's
PowerKids Press™
New York

To Mom and Dad

Published in 2007 by The Rosen Publishing Group, Inc.
29 East 21st Street, New York, NY 10010

First Edition

Editor: Kara Murray
Book Design: Elana Davidian

Photo Credits: Cover © Mitch York/Getty Images; p. 4 © Susan Findlay/Masterfile; p. 5 © Guy Grenier/Masterfile;
p. 10 © George Shelley/Corbis; p. 11 © Hal Beral/ zefa/Corbis; p. 13 © Mark E. Gibson/Corbis; p. 15 © Corbis; p. 19 © Alan Schein
Photography/Corbis; p. 21 © Alex Livesey/Getty Images.

Library of Congress Cataloging-in-Publication Data

Leech, Bonnie Coulter.
   Polygons / Bonnie Coulter Leech.— 1st ed.
      p. cm. — (The library of plane and solid geometric shapes)
   Includes index.
   ISBN 1-4042-3497-7
   1. Polygons—Juvenile literature. 2. Geometry, Plane—Juvenile literature. I. Title. II. Series.

   QA482.L4379 2007
   516'.154—dc22

                                            2005033444

Manufactured in the United States of America

Contents

Many things around you come in different shapes. Some shapes have many sides. For example, traffic signs come in different shapes. The different shapes have different numbers of sides. A stop sign has eight sides. Count them the next time you go for a ride. The speed limit, wrong way, and caution signs have four sides.

Most shapes around us are **three-dimensional** because they have length, **width**, and **height**. Take a look at your refrigerator.

Height

Width

Length

4

It has length and width, represented by the front and sides. It also has height, represented by how tall it is. However, if you draw a refrigerator on a sheet of paper, the drawing will have only length and width. The drawing will be flat. Shapes that have only length and width are **two-dimensional** shapes.

All traffic signs are two-dimensional shapes. How many of the signs shown here are four-sided shapes? How many signs have three sides? There is one sign that has eight sides. Can you find it?

Polygons

Shapes that have many sides are called polygons. Polygons are two-dimensional shapes because they have length and width but not height. Polygons are closed shapes. Place your finger on one point on a polygon. If you can trace around the shape and get back to the starting point without lifting your finger, then the shape is closed. There are no openings in a shape that is closed.

There are no curved lines in a polygon. The sides are straight line segments. A line segment is part of a line that has two endpoints. Each side of a polygon shares one endpoint with another side. The sides' endpoints are called **vertices**. One endpoint is called a vertex. Each vertex is a corner.

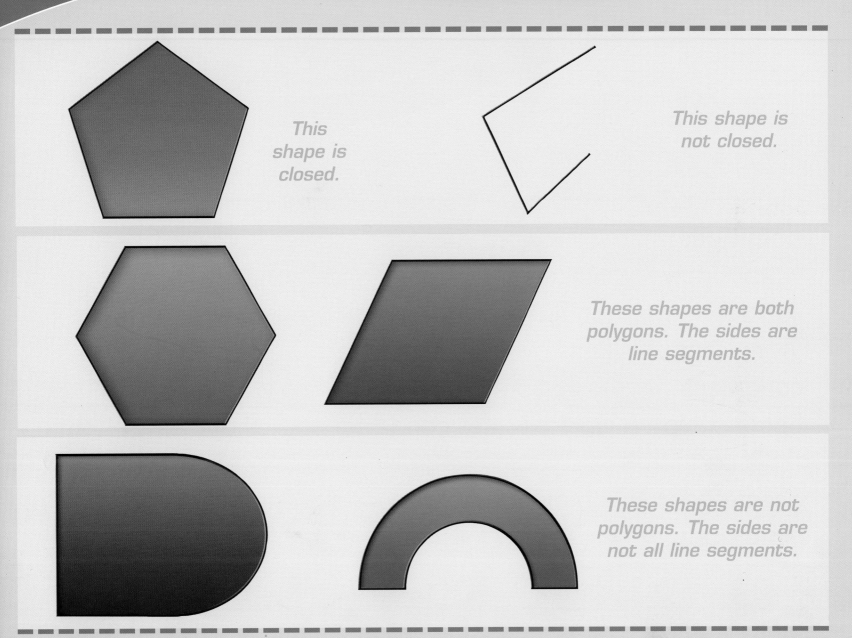

This shape is closed.

This shape is not closed.

These shapes are both polygons. The sides are line segments.

These shapes are not polygons. The sides are not all line segments.

When the sides of a polygon meet at a vertex, they form an angle. A polygon will have the same number of angles as it does sides. In fact the word "polygon" comes from the Greek words "poly," which means "many," and "gon," which means "angle." A polygon has many sides and many angles.

Line segments that have the same length are said to be **congruent**. Angles that are the same size are also congruent. Some polygons have all sides congruent and all angles congruent. These polygons are called regular polygons. In **geometry** when we are talking about polygons with five or more sides, we are usually talking about regular polygons.

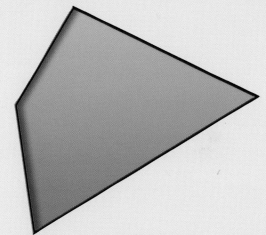

This polygon has four sides but is not a regular polygon.

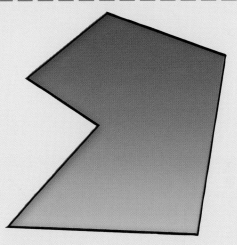

This polygon has six sides but is not a regular polygon.

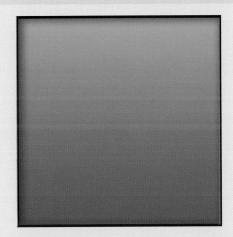

This four-sided shape is a regular polygon.

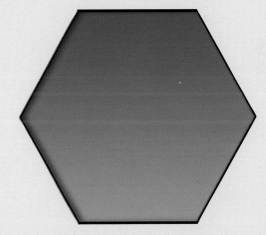

This six-sided shape is a regular polygon.

Polygons are **classified**, or given a name, by the number of sides and angles they have. The number of sides in a polygon is always the same as the number of angles. A **prefix** is used to name the number of sides and angles that the polygon has. A prefix is a part of a word that comes at the beginning, such as "bi-" or "tri-." If you put the prefix "bi-" or "tri-" in front of the word "cycle," you will form the word "bicycle" or "tricycle." A bicycle has two wheels and a tricycle has three wheels. Do you see how a prefix can help classify polygons?

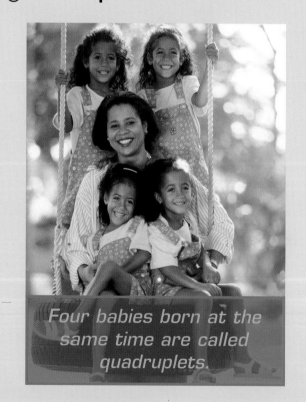

Four babies born at the same time are called quadruplets.

Look at other words that have prefixes. "Tri-" means "three." Three babies all born at the same time are called triplets. An octopus is an animal that has eight legs.

Can you find this octopus' eight legs? The word "octopus" comes from the prefix "octa-," which means "eight."

Prefix	Means	Shape
Tri-	3	Triangle
Quad-	4	Quadrilateral
Penta-	5	Pentagon
Hexa-	6	Hexagon
Hepta-	7	Heptagon
Octa-	8	Octagon
Nona-	9	Nonagon
Deca-	10	Decagon

The prefix in a polygon's name points out the number of sides and angles that the shape has. If a geometric shape has three sides and three angles, we can use the prefix "tri-" to name this shape. It is called a triangle because it has three angles. A triangle is named only for the number of angles that it has.

A geometric shape can also be named just for the number of sides that it has. One example is a quadrilateral. The word "lateral" means "side." Can you guess the number of sides a quadrilateral has by looking at the prefix? The prefix "quad-" means four. A quadrilateral has four sides.

These kids are playing a game called shuffleboard. The court on which the game is played is made up of triangles and quadrilaterals. Count the number of quadrilaterals on the court. Then count the triangles. How many did you find?

Pentagons

There are geometric shapes called pentagons. The prefix "penta-" means "five," and the suffix "-gon" means "angle." A suffix is a part of a word that comes at the end. A pentagon is a geometric shape with five angles and five sides. A regular pentagon has five sides that are all the same length and five angles that are all the same measure.

When we talk about pentagons or any other polygon, we give them a name using the letters at each vertex. Draw a pentagon. Place a capital letter at each vertex. Read the letters by starting at any vertex and continue reading the letters going either **clockwise** or **counterclockwise**.

Have you ever been to the Pentagon in Arlington, Virginia? The Pentagon is a building near Washington, D.C. The headquarters of the Department of Defense, which runs the U.S. military, is located there. Why do you think the building is called the Pentagon?

The Pentagon building is in the shape of a pentagon. Each of the Pentagon's sides measures 921 feet (281 m). The building is actually made up of four smaller pentagons inside a larger one.

Shapes that have six sides and six angles are called hexagons. The prefix "hexa-" means "six." If a shape has six sides that are line segments, and is closed, that shape is a hexagon. The figures below are both hexagons. Do you see the six sides?

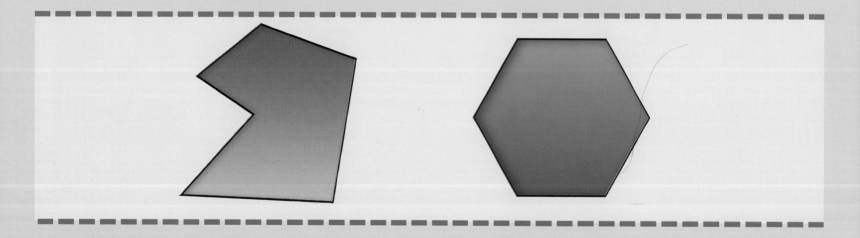

If the sides of a hexagon all have the same measure, then the hexagon is a regular hexagon. The distance around a hexagon or any polygon is called the perimeter.

In a regular hexagon, the perimeter can be found by measuring one side and then adding the measurement of that side six times. You could also multiply the number of sides in a hexagon by the length of one side to find the perimeter. This is true for all regular polygons.

The perimeter of regular hexagon ABCDEF is 3 + 3 + 3 + 3 + 3 + 3 or 3 x 6. The perimeter is 18 cm.

3 cm

Geometric figures that have eight sides and eight angles are called octagons. The prefix "octa-" means "eight." The eight sides of an octagon are line segments. A shape with eight sides that may be **familiar** to you is a stop sign. Any

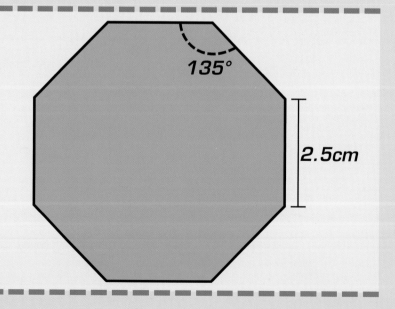

This is a regular octagon. Each of its angles measures 135°, and each of its sides measures 2.5 cm. Since there are eight sides, the perimeter of this octagon is 2.5 x 8, or 20 cm.

135°

2.5cm

two-dimensional, closed shape with eight sides is an octagon. The figure shown on page 18 is an octagon. Do you see the eight sides?

As all regular polygons do, all sides of regular octagons have the same measure. The angles of an octagon are all the same size. To find the perimeter of a regular octagon, measure one side. Then multiply the measurement of the side by eight.

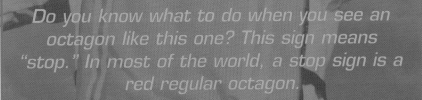

Do you know what to do when you see an octagon like this one? This sign means "stop." In most of the world, a stop sign is a red regular octagon.

A geometric figure that has ten sides is called a decagon. A decagon is a two-dimensional, closed shape. Like all regular polygons, a regular decagon has **symmetry**. If a shape is symmetrical, you can fold that shape in half and both sides will match.

The prefix "deca-" comes from the Greek word *deka*, which means "ten." There are many things around us that come in tens. We have 10 fingers and 10 toes. There are 10 dimes in a dollar. There are 10 years in a **decade**. During the Summer Olympics, **athletes** take part in the **decathlon**. A decathlon is a **competition** that has 10 events.

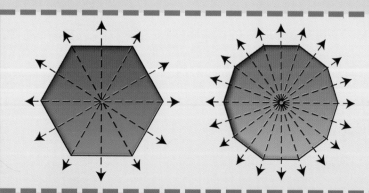

A regular decagon, like the one shown here, has 10 lines of symmetry. A hexagon has six lines of symmetry. Any regular polygon will have the same number of lines of symmetry as it has angles and sides.

This athlete is taking part in the long jump. The long jump is one of the 10 events in the decathlon.

Polygons, such as triangles, quadrilaterals, and hexagons, can be seen in many objects around your home. The tiles on your floors and walls might be quadrilaterals. Windows, doors, and beds are also in the shape of quadrilaterals. A soccer ball has a pattern made up of pentagons and hexagons on it. Artwork and rugs and pictures may use many different polygons. Many polygons are used together in a **tangram**. A tangram is a seven-piece puzzle made of paper, foam, or wood. A tangram consists of seven polygons. Tangrams contain five triangles, one quadrilateral, and one square. The pieces of the puzzle can be put together to make shapes that look like different objects, such as birds and frogs. Tangrams are just one of the many ways that we can make use of different polygons.

Glossary

athletes (ATH-leets) People who take part in sports.

classified (KLA-seh-fyd) Arranged in groups.

clockwise (KLOK-wyz) Moving in the direction that the hands of a clock move.

competition (kom-pih-TIH-shun) A game or test.

congruent (kun-GROO-ent) Having the same measurement and shape.

counterclockwise (kown-ter-KLOK-wyz) Moving in the opposite direction that the hands of a clock move.

decade (DEH-kayd) A period of time consisting of 10 years.

decathlon (dih-KATH-lon) A sporting contest consisting of 10 events.

familiar (fuh-MIL-yer) Something or someone that is well known, common.

geometry (jee-AH-meh-tree) A type of math that deals with straight lines, circles, and other shapes.

height (HYT) The distance from the top to the bottom of a shape.

prefix (PREE-fiks) A group of letters that comes at the beginning of a word and that has meaning of its own.

symmetry (SIH-muh-tree) Meaning that something is equally balanced.

tangram (TAN-gram) A Chinese puzzle made of seven pieces.

three-dimensional (three-deh-MENCH-nul) Having height, width, and length.

two-dimensional (too-deh-MENCH-nul) Able to be measured two ways, by length and by width.

vertices (VER-tuh-seez) The points where two lines or line segments meet.

width (WITH) The measure of how wide a figure is.

Index

Web Sites

Due to the changing nature of Internet links, PowerKids Press has developed an online list of Web sites related to the subject of this book. This site is updated regularly. Please use this link to access the list:

www.powerkidslinks.com/psgs/polygons/